BY JAKE MADDOX

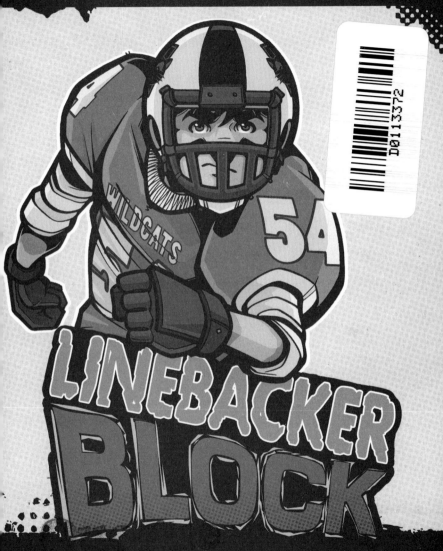

LINEBACKER BLOCK

ILLUSTRATED BY SEAN TIFFANY

text by Eric Stevens

STONE ARCH BOOKS
a capstone imprint

Impact Books are published by Stone Arch Books
A Capstone Imprint
151 Good Counsel Drive, P.O. Box 669
Mankato, Minnesota 56002
www.capstonepub.com

Printed in the United States of America in Stevens Point, Wisconsin.
032010
005741WZF10

Library of Congress Cataloging-in-Publication Data
Maddox, Jake.
  Linebacker block / by Jake Maddox ; text by Eric Stevens ; illustrated by Sean
Tiffany.
    p. cm. -- (Impact books: a Jake Maddox sports story)
  ISBN 978-1-4342-1635-9 (library binding), 978-1-4342-2779-9 (paperback)
  [1. Football--Fiction.] I. Stevens, Eric, 1974- II. Tiffany, Sean, ill. III. Title.
  PZ7.M25643Lin 2010
  [Fic]--dc22
                                        2010006271

Art Director: Kay Fraser
Graphic Designer: Hilary Wacholz
Production Specialist: Michelle Biedscheid

Photo Credits: ShutterStock/Mike Flippo (p. 2, 3, 5)

WILDCATS FOOTB

E HUSKIE
CYCLONE
HALES
LIONS
CCANEE
ES
ES
ARS
IS
CANEE

TABLE OF CONTENTS

Playbook of Defense Techniques

ANDREW, LOGAN, COACH FRENCH, NOAH, CARLOS

OCT. 13 VS. EASTLAKE EAGLES

OCT. 20 VS. WHEATON WHALES

OCT. 27 VS. HORTONTON HUSKIES

NOV. 3 VS. LISBON LIONS

NOV. VS. BLOOMBERY BUCCANEERS

HOME ALONE

The sun was going down on a Saturday evening in Westfield. Most of the eighth graders were out with their friends, down at Taco Paco's, at the movie theater on the north side of town, or maybe just hanging out at someone's house, playing video games.

But Logan Meltzer was alone. He was sitting in the TV room in the basement of his house.

He had the remote control in his right hand and was flipping through all one hundred and fifty-eight channels at blinding speed.

A news show. A boring music video. Cartoons. Something in Japanese. A lady cooking fish. A man in a boat, fishing.

In other words, nothing was on.

Logan heard someone coming. The *thud-thud-thud* of someone on the steps got louder and louder. Logan knew it had to be his dad.

"Logan!" his dad's voice called. The door to the TV room opened.

Logan's father was a very big man. In fact, Logan took after his dad, which was one of the reasons Logan was a good linebacker.

Logan's dad was over six feet tall, and weighed about three hundred pounds. When he walked into the room, he huffed from his nose. Logan always thought it made him look like a bull.

"Logan, what are you doing down here all alone?" his dad asked.

"What does it look like I'm doing?" Logan said. He glanced at his father, then back at the TV. "I'm watching TV."

His dad sighed and then dropped down on the couch next to Logan. He put his big hand onto Logan's shoulder and gave it a couple of pats.

"I'm worried about you, Logan," his dad said. "Back in River City, you would never be home alone, flipping through the channels — not on a Saturday night!"

Logan kept pushing buttons on the remote, barely stopping for an instant to see what was what. "That's easy for you to say," Logan said. "You and Mom are going out tonight with your friends from River City. I can't, because I can't drive back to River City whenever I feel like it."

Logan's dad nodded. "I know," he said. "It doesn't seem fair."

"Yeah. Because it isn't fair," Logan pointed out.

His dad groaned and rubbed his neck. "Logan, we've been over this," he said. "It will get easier. What about the guys on the football team?"

Logan shrugged and looked at his dad. "What about the guys on the team?" he repeated.

"Don't those guys go out on a Saturday night?" his dad said. "Maybe to a movie, or to the skating rink, or something?"

"The skating rink?" Logan said with a laugh. "Dad, come on."

"I don't know!" his dad replied, shrugging. "When I was young, we went roller-skating. What do I know?"

"Not much," Logan said, smiling. "Well, I guess I can be glad I don't have to play against my old team. We're not playing River City this season. I checked the schedule."

"Good, good," his dad said. "And listen. This will get easier for you, Logan. You'll get to know the kids in school and on the team. You won't be stuck at home on Saturdays for much longer, I promise."

Logan nodded. "I know," he said. "Hey, I'm going to send an email to Scotty Hansen back home."

He got up from the couch and clicked the TV off. "I mean," he added quickly, "back in River City."

His dad laughed and headed up the steps.

CHAPTER 2

OLD FRIENDS

After school on Monday, Logan plodded down the hall toward the locker room. The football team had practice every day after school. Logan pushed through the locker room door and sat on the bench in front of his locker.

At least I have the football team, Logan thought as he pulled open his locker. He put on his pads for practice and found his practice jersey in the back of his locker.

He picked it up and gave it a sniff. He wrinkled up his nose at the stench. "Oops," he said aloud.

Someone laughed as Logan turned around. It was Andrew, a wide receiver. "Forgot to bring that home to wash it, huh?" Andrew asked.

Logan smiled. "Yeah, I guess," he said. But he couldn't tell if Andrew was making fun of him or just being friendly. It was hard to tell. Andrew laughed again and then walked off toward his own locker.

Logan wrinkled his nose as he put on his smelly jersey. Then he grabbed his helmet and headed out to the field. Most of the team was already gathered on the sidelines, on or around the bench. The coach, Greg French, stood in front of the guys on the team.

Coach was in his blue and white Wildcats jacket, and he was wearing his blue and white Wildcats hat, like always. He also always had a whistle around his neck, and he was usually holding a clipboard.

"Okay, everyone," the coach said. Logan found an empty spot at the very end of the bench and sat down.

Everyone was talking, and no one paid attention to the coach. Luckily, Coach French was a nice guy, who always let the players have a few minutes to hang out before practice started.

"Let's quiet down, okay?" Coach French went on. "I need to announce some changes to the schedule for the week."

The team got quiet.

WILDCATS FOOTBALL
SEPT. 8 VS. HORTONVILLE HUSKIES
SEPT. 15 VS. RIVER CITY CYCLONES
SEPT. 22 VS. WHEATON WHALES
SEPT. 29 VS. LYNNESBURG LIONS
OCT. 6 VS. BLOOMFIELD BUCCANEERS
OCT. 13 VS. EASTLAKE EAGLES
OCT. 20 VS. WHEATON WHALES
OCT. 27 VS. HORTON

"So, this Friday's game," the coach said, "has been changed. It seems that some teams were playing each other too often, or not often enough. I don't know what happened."

He looked down at his clipboard and flipped through the papers. "The point is," he said, looking up at the team, "this Friday we'll be playing River City, not Wheaton."

Logan's eyes shot open. He thought he might throw up.

The coach looked right at him. "That's where you moved from, Logan. Isn't that right?" Coach French asked.

Logan swallowed and nodded. "Right, Coach," he said. "I played on the River City team last year, in seventh grade."

All of the other players turned and looked at him.

"So, can we count on you to tell us all their secret plays?" the coach asked. He looked at Logan with a hard stare.

Logan stared at him. All of a sudden, he wondered if Coach French wasn't as nice as he'd thought. "Um, well . . ." he mumbled.

Suddenly the coach burst out laughing. "I'm just kidding, Logan," he said, smiling. "Don't worry!"

The rest of the team started laughing too, and Logan tried to smile. But inside, he felt terrible. It seemed like his new team was making fun of him. To make matters worse, in a few days, he'd have to play football against his old teammates — his best friends!

CHAPTER 3

MEATLOAF

Logan walked really slowly on the way home from school that day. His body was sore from practice, but mainly he was feeling down.

Even though his family's house wasn't far from the school, it took him almost an hour to get home.

"Logan!" his mother called when he walked in. "You're so late!"

She came out of the kitchen. She was still in her suit from work, but she was also wearing oven mitts on both hands.

Logan's mom was a tiny woman, not more than five feet tall, and she looked like a strong breeze would knock her over. When she and Logan's dad hugged or danced, Logan always thought she might get crushed.

"Sorry, Mom," Logan said. He followed her back into the kitchen.

His dad was waiting at the table. "Hi, Dad. Sorry I'm late," said Logan.

His dad shrugged his big shoulders. "You're just in time for supper," he said, "so no harm done."

Logan sat down and watched as his mom put a meatloaf on the table.

The meatloaf wasn't homemade. It was in an aluminum foil pan.

"Frozen meatloaf, huh?" Logan asked.

His dad chuckled and started slicing the meatloaf. "It's great," he said. "I lived on this frozen meatloaf in college."

The meatloaf turned out to be not too bad. Soon, Logan was stuffed full.

"Any plans tonight?" Dad asked as Logan cleared the table.

Logan shook his head. "Nope. I'm just going to do my homework and hang out here, I guess," he said. Then he headed downstairs.

He sat down at the computer desk and switched it on. He was hoping he'd have an email back from his friend Scotty, and sure enough, he did.

Hey, Logan!

What's up? Not much is new here. Wish you were still around to hang out with.

So you probably heard by now that the Cyclones are playing your team on Friday. They changed the schedule!

How cool is that? I thought we weren't going to a get a chance to play any ball together this year, but it looks like we will after all.

I'm pretty excited. See you on Friday afternoon!

Scotty

Logan clicked "reply," but then just stared at the blank email. What could he say? He wasn't excited about the game at all. In fact, it was tearing him apart.

So, instead of typing anything, he just closed the blank email and flicked off the monitor. Then he dropped onto the couch and started flipping through the TV channels again.

CHAPTER 4

NEW RIVALS

At lunch on Friday, Logan was waiting in line in the cafeteria. It was pizza day, like every Friday. Logan tapped his fingers on his tray as he waited.

"Hey, Logan," someone said behind him. Logan turned.

It was Andrew again, the wide receiver from the football team.

"Oh, hi, Andrew," Logan said.

Andrew smacked his lips. "Man, I love pizza day," he said. He peeked around Logan to get a look at the line. "What's taking so long up there?" he called out. "I want my lunch!"

The woman behind the counter waved at him. "You keep it down, Andrew," she said, smiling. "You'll get your lunch."

Andrew laughed and then looked at Logan. "So we're playing your old team in a few hours, huh?" he asked.

Logan nodded. "Yeah," he said. "The River City Cyclones."

The line inched up slowly.

"Is that going to be weird?" Andrew asked. "I mean, I can't imagine having to play against the guys on the Wildcats. And all I have to do is run and catch."

"What do you mean? Why would it be weird?" Logan asked. "Playing is playing."

They had reached the food. Logan got two square pieces of pizza. He also took a bowl of vanilla pudding and a bowl of peas and carrots.

Andrew turned to the server and smiled. "I want four slices, Carol," he said. "Let me have four slices."

Carol, the server, laughed. "Hey, Andrew," she said, "if you're paying for two lunches, you're getting two lunches." She gave him the four slices he'd asked for and laughed again.

The two of them walked to the cash register and paid. "Why would it be weird to play against my old team?" Logan asked again.

"Well," Andrew said as they left the line and headed toward the tables, "you'll be rushing their quarterback, going after their running backs . . . you know, tackling them. I don't know, I think that would be pretty tough."

Andrew shook his head and headed to the table at the far side of the room, where the whole football team was having lunch. When Logan didn't follow him, Andrew turned around.

"Hey, man," Andrew said. "Why don't you come over and eat lunch with the rest of the team today? Just because you're the new guy doesn't mean you have to eat lunch alone."

Logan looked down at his pizza. He thought about what Andrew had said.

Logan was going to have to play against his old friends. He'd have to do his best to make sure the River City quarterback couldn't complete a single pass. Even worse, Scotty was a running back. He'd have to tackle Scotty.

Logan looked back at Andrew, who was standing there waiting for him.

"Actually, um," Logan said, "I'm supposed to be meeting with Mr. Goulet, um, about my French class project. So I better head to his office."

That was a lie. Logan just couldn't bring himself to have lunch with his new football team. It felt like he was cheating on a friend.

Andrew squinted at Logan. "Okay," he said. "Sounds like fun."

Logan shrugged. "Yeah," he said, heading to the door. "I don't have a choice though, I guess."

He quickly left the cafeteria, carrying his tray of lunch. He headed for the library, where he hid in a corner to eat his pizza. It felt like rocks in his stomach.

CHAPTER 5

THE
FIRST HALF

That afternoon, Logan sat on the Wildcats bench. The special team took the field to receive the first kickoff.

It was still weird for Logan to watch his own team come onto the field in blue and white. He wasn't used to the uniform or the team name. When the Cyclones took the field, he felt his spirits rise watching the players, with their familiar maroon jerseys and the silver tornado logo on their helmets.

Logan watched the start of the game from the bench. He was very glad his team had the ball first, not because it was an advantage, but because it meant he wouldn't have to take the field for a little while.

The Cyclones defense wasn't bad, he decided, although he was almost sorry to admit it.

They don't seem to be missing me, he thought as he watched.

On third down, a huge hole opened in the Wildcats offensive line. *I easily could have gotten through there if I were still on the Cyclones*, he thought.

But his old teammates missed the chance. The Wildcats connected a twenty-yard pass and got a first down.

On the bench, the other defensive players cheered. Logan didn't even think about cheering. For a moment, he had forgotten which team he was on.

When Logan didn't get up, the others looked at him, and he felt stupid. Logan decided to make up for it. He clapped his hands and shouted, "Good job, offense! Keep it up!" But then he felt even stupider for being so late with his cheer.

Logan frowned. *Whatever*, he thought. *We shouldn't have completed that pass anyway, with that weak blocking.*

The Wildcats scored a touchdown on the drive and got the extra point. When Logan took the field after the kickoff, his team was winning 7-0.

* * *

Logan stood behind the defensive line. As a linebacker, he started standing, while the linemen started bent over with one hand on the grass. That way, Logan could see over the line and call out to the other players what the offense might be planning.

On first down, Logan spotted some motion. He called out to his teammates to watch for the run to the left side.

Then he spotted the Cyclones running back's number and name on his jersey. It was his friend Scotty Hansen.

"Hut, hut!" the Cyclones quarterback shouted. "Hike!" And he took the snap. Right away, he turned to his right and handed off to Scotty.

Scotty shot toward the left side and then cut up the field. Logan moved in to close off the hole in his defensive line, but Scotty spun and got around him. Logan ended up on the grass. He watched Scotty make a ten-yard run. One of the other Wildcat linebackers finally got him down at the forty.

Logan got to his feet. Suddenly Scotty was next to him. He was smiling and out of breath.

"Hey, Logan," he said. "Are you out of shape or something?"

Logan looked at him. "What do you mean?" he asked.

"I could never get past you in scrimmages last year," Scotty said. "Either you're out of shape, or I've gotten much better."

Logan tried to laugh as Scotty patted him on the pads and walked to the River City huddle. But then Logan turned and saw one of the other defensive players from the Wildcats.

"Hey, James," Logan said. But James only glared at him, then walked off.

Great, Logan thought. *He probably thinks I let Scotty get by because he's my friend.*

But then Logan wondered if he really had tried as hard as he could. The truth was, he didn't know.

CHAPTER 6

The Cyclones' drive up the field
continued to go well. Logan tried hard to
stop their forward motion. But every time
he saw a guy from River City catching the
ball, or running with it, he felt torn.

*Why did this game have to be against River
City?* he asked himself. *Why couldn't we play
against a different team, a team that wasn't
made up of my best friends? Trying to beat
strangers would be way easier.*

The Cyclones were lined up at the Wildcats' thirty-yard line. It was third down. On this play, if the defense could stop them, the Cyclones would have their last chance for six points. It was up to the defense to keep them to three points at most.

"Hut!" the Cyclones quarterback shouted. "Hike!"

The Cyclones center snapped the ball. Logan watched the quarterback pull back. He faked the handoff to Scotty, who went out wide to the right. Logan saw the screen pass just before it happened. He sprinted through a hole in the line as the pass left the quarterback's hand.

Then suddenly Logan felt worried. *I can't intercept a pass to Scotty,* he thought. *He's my best friend!*

Logan slowed down. He didn't really mean to. It just happened. At the last second, he leaped for the ball, hoping everyone would see how hard he was trying. But he knew it was too late. The perfect pass sailed over his fingertips and Scotty caught it.

Logan sprawled out on the grass and lifted his head. He was just able to get to his feet in time to watch his old friend — and new rival — run into the end zone for six points.

River City would tie it up with the extra point. Logan knew he could have stopped them. But did he want to?

CHAPTER 7

BAD DAY

Logan jogged over to the bench. Andrew was putting on his helmet, getting ready for the offense's turn on the field.

"Hey, Logan," he said. "You seem pretty slow out there today."

Logan swallowed. "I do?" he asked. But he knew it was true.

"Yeah," Andrew replied. "Are you feeling all right?" He didn't wait for an answer.

"Maybe Otis can come in for you," Andrew went on. "I'm sure he'd like the chance to play. We can talk to the coach if you need a rest." Andrew patted Logan's shoulder pads.

"No, I'm fine," Logan said.

Andrew shrugged and headed out to the field, while Logan dropped onto the bench, feeling miserable.

The Wildcats offense had another good drive. Andrew made an excellent catch on second down and took the ball all the way to the Cyclones' forty-yard line. Everyone on the bench went crazy. Even Logan got up and cheered.

Everyone sure is playing hard, he thought. He wished it were as easy for him to pick a side.

On the next few plays, the Cyclones' defense was very strong, and the Wildcats were forced to kick the field goal. That gave them the lead going into halftime. But with the score at 10-7, the Wildcats were only up by three points.

If Logan and the defense couldn't stop the Cyclones, River City would easily tie it up. They could even take the lead.

CHAPTER 8

HALFTIME

The feeling in the locker room didn't match the feeling in Logan's stomach. Everyone was in a great mood. After all, they were up by three points. A few players on the offense were having a really good game so far. Everyone was pretty sure that they'd win the game.

But Logan felt sick. A small part of his brain kept thinking, *If it weren't for me, we'd be up by ten points!*

"Everyone settle down, all right?" the coach said. The players all took a seat on a bench or leaned against the lockers or walls.

Logan stood toward the back of the group and looked at his feet. He watched the other members of the team high-five each other as they started to quiet down. Finally Coach French blew his whistle and the room fell silent.

"I'm glad you're all excited," the coach said with a smile, "but as far as I can tell, we still have half this game to go."

A few players mumbled in reply.

"And we're only up by three points," the coach added. "So don't get too confident, and don't think we have this game in the bag, okay?"

"Okay, Coach," the team replied all together.

"All right," Coach French said. He nodded. "Now then, let's go over a few things. . . ."

Logan didn't pay very close attention as the coach rattled off some plays that hadn't worked well and mentioned some defensive mistakes. He felt like he didn't need to hear about those. After all, those mistakes had been his fault!

When the coach was done with his speech, he found Logan.

"Logan, I noticed you seem a little sluggish out there," Coach French said. "I've seen you block tougher passes in practice than that screen on the Cyclones' first drive."

"I really went for it, Coach," Logan said. "I just missed it. The pass went right past my fingertips."

The coach looked at him a second. "Okay, Logan," he said. "As long as you're giving it your all."

He patted Logan on the shoulder and walked off, looking down at his clipboard. Then Logan saw that Andrew had been standing behind the coach. He had overheard the conversation.

"I guess Coach noticed the same thing I did, huh?" Andrew asked.

"Man!" Logan said. "I wish you'd stop giving me such a hard time. So I'm having a bad day, and my jersey stinks because I forgot to wash it, and I eat lunch alone! So what?"

Andrew took a step back and smiled. "Whoa, whoa," he said, putting his hands up. "Take it easy. I didn't mean to make you angry."

Logan took a deep breath. "Sorry," he said. "I guess I'm having kind of a rough game."

"So what's the problem?" Andrew asked.

"Isn't it obvious?" Logan said. "The guys on the Cyclones — some of them are my best friends. Their running back, Scotty Hansen, used to come over to my house after school almost every day, because his mom worked late. We went to school together for eight years. We grew up together. And we've played ball together since we were like, five. How am I supposed to play against him?"

"Oh, I hear you," Andrew replied. "I don't think I'd like having to play football against the guys on the Wildcats."

"Exactly," Logan said, shaking his head.

Andrew glanced up at the game clock. The second half was about to start.

"We should get out there," Andrew said. "But you know what?"

Logan looked at the linebacker. "What?" he asked.

"I think maybe it isn't about being a bad friend," Andrew said. "Because really all of us are just out here because we love playing football, right?"

"Right," Logan replied. "I guess that's why I've always played. Scotty too. He loves the game."

"And the truth is, if you're not trying to stop Hansen from running the ball or catching that screen pass," Andrew went on, "then Hansen doesn't get to play real football."

Andrew pushed open the doors to the field. "He might as well go play with the peewee league," he added. "Know what I mean?"

Logan nodded as he walked through the door. "Yeah," he said. "I know exactly what you mean."

CHAPTER 9

SECOND HALF

The second half started with the Wildcats kicking off to the Cyclones. That meant Logan was on the field in his two-point stance almost right away.

Logan stood tall over the line. He spotted Scotty in motion.

"Watch for the handoff," Logan shouted to his teammates.

"Hike!" called the Cyclones quarterback.

Scotty came running up behind him and went for the handoff. But the quarterback faked and drew back from the pocket.

"He's passing!" Logan called out. He spotted Scotty running fast toward the left sideline, and he ran after him.

"Screen left!" Logan shouted to his line. Two of the other linemen pulled back from rushing the quarterback and chased Scotty just as the pass was released.

But Logan was even quicker. He wasn't close enough to intercept, but he launched through the air and got one finger on the ball. It was enough to send it tumbling to the grass.

"Nice block, Logan!" another linemen called out. He felt a few hands pat his helmet and smiled.

"Nice one, Logan," a familiar voice said. It was Scotty. He was smiling, too. "Glad to see you came out to play today. Finally."

Scotty jogged back to his own team's huddle. Logan lined up with the defenders.

That's right, he thought. *I am here to play.*

"All right, D," he shouted to his teammates, clapping his hands. "Let's keep 'em stopped right here."

The other defensive players hooted and clapped with him. And Logan finally felt like he was on the right team.

CHAPTER 10

NEW FRIENDS

Logan's defensive line was really giving it their all for the whole second half. In fact, not a single Cyclone drive reached a first-down marker. When the referee blew the whistle for the two-minute warning, the Wildcats were up by ten points.

Logan watched his team march up the field from the bench. He clapped and hollered along with everyone else after every complete pass and every run.

Coach French walked over and patted Logan's helmet. "You've really improved in this second half, Logan," the coach said. "Maybe good enough for today's MVP award. You must be warmed up."

"Sort of," Logan replied. "It was something Andrew said to me before the second half started. Kind of gave me my energy back."

"Well, remind me to make him MVP, then," the coach said with a laugh. "Keep up the good work out there. You're doing great."

* * *

In the end, the Wildcats won 24-7. And just like he'd said he would, after the game, Coach French named Logan the MVP of the game.

Logan finished showering and changing and was heading out of the locker room when Andrew walked up to him. The Wildcats quarterback, Carlos, was there too.

"You guys, we should go out and celebrate," Andrew said. "Let's go down to Paco's and get some tacos and then catch a movie or something."

"Definitely!" Carlos said. "Logan, I can't remember the last time someone on the defensive squad got MVP."

Logan smiled. "That sounds good," he said as the three boys reached the parking lot. Then he spotted someone across the pavement.

"Hey, Scotty!" Logan called out.

His old friend from River City waved. Logan called him over.

"Why don't you join us for some tacos," Logan said. "And then maybe we can catch that new horror movie."

Scotty looked from Logan to Carlos and to Andrew. "Um, sure," Scotty said. "Okay."

Andrew laughed. "Man, don't worry," he said. "We're all just playing football. It doesn't mean we have to hate each other."

Logan nodded. "That's right," he said. "Which is why, even though I don't hate you and the other guys on the Cyclones, we still beat you guys today."

Carlos and Andrew cracked up laughing.

Scotty smiled. "Ha ha," he said. "You're just lucky you won't have to face us again this season."

The three Wildcats laughed at that too.

Logan looked around. On one side, he had an old friend from River City. On the other side, he had two new friends, from the Wildcats.

We all love football, he thought. *And I'm starting to love my school.*

As the sun went down behind the water tower, the four friends headed down the road to Taco Paco's.

THE AUTHOR
ERIC STEVENS

15

ERIC STEVENS LIVES IN ST. PAUL, MINNESOTA WITH HIS WIFE, DOG, AND SON. HE IS STUDYING TO BECOME A TEACHER. SOME OF HIS FAVORITE THINGS INCLUDE PIZZA AND VIDEO GAMES. SOME OF HIS LEAST FAVORITE THINGS INCLUDE OLIVES AND SHOVELING SNOW.

24

THE ILLUSTRATOR
SEAN TIFFANY

WHEN SEAN TIFFANY WAS GROWING UP, HE LIVED ON A SMALL ISLAND OFF THE COAST OF MAINE. EVERY DAY UNTIL HE GRADUATED FROM HIGH SCHOOL, HE HAD TO TAKE A BOAT TO GET TO SCHOOL! SEAN HAS A PET CACTUS NAMED JIM.

GLOSSARY

advantage (ad-VAN-tij)—something that helps or is useful to you

announce (uh-NOUNSS)—to say something publicly

confident (KON-fuh-duhnt)—having a strong belief in your own abilities

familiar (fuh-MIL-yur)—something you know well

intercept (in-tur-SEPT)—to stop the movement of something

miserable (MIZ-ur-uh-buhl)—sad, unhappy

motion (MOH-shuhn)—movement

schedule (SKEJ-ool)—a plan

scrimmages (SKRIM-ij-iz)—games played for practice

stance (STANSS)—the way someone stands

DISCUSSION QUESTIONS

1. What are some ways to make friends when you go to a new school or move to a new place?

2. Was Andrew picking on Logan in this book? Explain your answer.

3. Coach French awarded Logan the MVP award. Do you think Logan deserved it? Why or why not?

WRITING PROMPTS

1. Pretend you're Logan. Write an e-mail to your friend Scotty, telling him about your new house, school, and football team.

2. What happens after this book ends? Write a chapter that continues the story.

3. Write about a time you had to make new friends. What did you do? How did you feel?

MORE ABOUT LINEBACKERS

In this book, Logan Meltzer is a linebacker for the Westfield Wildcats. Check out these quick facts about linebackers.

- Linebackers are key members of the defensive team of a football team.

- A linebacker's job is to defend his team's goal and protect passes. He needs to be strong enough to tackle players on the opposing team, so that he can stop the other side from scoring points.

- The position of linebacker is said to have been invented by legendary football coach Fielding Yost, who coached at the University of Michigan for more than two decades.

- Some famous linebackers have included Dick Butkus, Mike Singletary, Brian Urlacher, and Lawrence Taylor.

THE WILDCATS

FIND THESE AND OTHER JAKE MADDOX BOOKS AT
WWW.CAPSTONEPUB.COM